THE SENSUALIST

Ruskin Bond's first novel, *The Room on the Roof*, written when he was seventeen, won the John Llewellyn Rhys Memorial Prize in 1957. Since then he has written several novellas (including *Vagrants in the Valley*, *A Flight of Pigeons* and *Delhi Is Not Far*), essays, poems and children's books, many of which have been published by Penguin India. He has also written over 500 short stories and articles that have appeared in a number of magazines and anthologies. He received the Sahitya Akademi Award in 1993 and the Padma Shri in 1999.

Ruskin Bond was born in Kasauli, Himachal Pradesh, and grew up in Jamnagar, Dehradun, Delhi and Shimla. As a young man, he spent four years in the Channel Islands and London. He returned to India in 1955 and has never left the country since. He now lives in Landour, Mussoorie, with his adopted family.

ALSO BY RUSKIN BOND

Fiction
The Room on the Roof & Vagrants in the Valley
The Night Train at Deoli and Other Stories
Time Stops at Shamli and Other Stories
Our Trees Still Grow in Dehra
A Season of Ghosts
When Darkness Falls and Other Stories
A Flight of Pigeons
Delhi Is Not Far
A Face in the Dark and Other Hauntings
The Sensualist
A Handful of Nuts

Non-fiction
Rain in the Mountains
Scenes from a Writer's Life
The Lamp Is Lit
The Little Book of Comfort
Landour Days
Notes from a Small Room

Anthologies
Dust on the Mountain: Collected Stories
The Best of Ruskin Bond
Friends in Small Places
Indian Ghost Stories (ed.)
Indian Railway Stories (ed.)
Classical Indian Love Stories and Lyrics (ed.)
Tales of the Open Road
Ruskin Bond's Book of Nature
Ruskin Bond's Book of Humour
A Town Called Dehra

Poetry
Ruskin Bond's Book of Verse

The Sensualist

RUSKIN BOND

PENGUIN BOOKS

PENGUIN BOOKS
Published by the Penguin Group
Penguin Books India Pvt. Ltd, 7th Floor, Infinity Tower C,
DLF Cyber City, Gurgaon 122 002, Haryana, India
Penguin Group (USA) Inc., 375 Hudson Street, New York,
New York 10014, USA
Penguin Group (Canada), 90 Eglinton Avenue East, Suite 700, Toronto,
Ontario, M4P 2Y3, Canada
Penguin Books Ltd, 80 Strand, London WC2R 0RL, England
Penguin Ireland, 25 St Stephen's Green, Dublin 2, Ireland (a division of
Penguin Books Ltd)
Penguin Group (Australia), 707 Collins Street, Melbourne, Victoria 3008,
Australia
Penguin Group (NZ), 67 Apollo Drive, Rosedale, Auckland 0632,
New Zealand
Penguin Books (South Africa) (Pty) Ltd, Block D, Rosebank Office Park,
181 Jan Smuts Avenue, Parktown North, Johannesburg 2193, South Africa

Penguin Books Ltd, Registered Offices: 80 Strand, London WC2R 0RL,
England

Published as part of *Strangers in the Night: Two Novellas* 1996
This edition first published by Penguin Books India 2009

ISBN 9780143067412

Typeset in Goudy Old Style CGATT by SÜRYA, New Delhi
Printed at Repro India Ltd, Navi Mumbai

A PENGUIN RANDOM HOUSE COMPANY

Author's Note

Let it be said at the outset that this book is not intended for the school classroom.

Over the years, a number of my stories, some of them written especially for young readers, have found their way into the school or college curriculum, both in India and elsewhere. I have always enjoyed this aspect of my work. But that does not mean I must never write for adults, or that I should refrain from crossing the borderlands of physical passion and human desire. Just now and then I let my hair down and indulge in a little gentle ribaldry or a tale of desire under the deodars.

But you can relax dear reader. I am not about to offer you a plateful of porn. *The Sensualist* is the story of a man enslaved by an overpowering sex-drive, but it takes him on the downward spiralling road to self-destruction; you could even say it has a moral.

The Sensualist is a novella or long short story, a form that seems to suit my style and temperament. Only the French (and occasionally the Americans) have really done justice to the novella. The British prefer the proliferation of the longer novel, and British publishers won't look at a novella; they want their money's worth of words. But the short novel, with its compositional economy and homogeneity of conception, has its place in the scheme of things, as Conrad demonstrated in *Heart of Darkness*, *The Shadow-Line*, *Youth* and *The Nigger of Narcissus*. But he was a Pole writing in English. Andre Gide's *The Immoralist* was also a strong early influence.

Although I cannot aspire to being another Conrad, something from the Master may have rubbed off on me. In *The Sensualist* there is a certain brooding quality and a pessimism which is alien to my nature. I have also used the device of a narrative within a narrative. The recluse in the mountains is my other self, my 'secret sharer'. But *The Sensualist* is not in any way autobiographical. There is a Jekyll and Hyde in each of us, two personalities warring with each other, and to that extent it reveals something of the author's psyche. 'Interesting if true,' said Mark Twain in a different context. 'And if not true, still interesting.'

The Sensualist was written more than three decades ago, and first appeared in the Bombay magazine *Debonair*, where it was serialized over three or four issues. One summer's day, while I was enjoying the shade of a maple tree outside my Mussoorie home, a policeman appeared before me with a warrant for my arrest. It was a non-bailable warrant. The policeman was not from the local station. He had come all the way from Bombay to apprehend me. There was an obscenity charge hanging over me in that fair city, and the warrant declared that I was absconding from the law. That was the time of the Emergency (1975–76), and writers and journalists were being given a rough time. *Debonair* had just been taken over by Vinod Mehta and he was greeted with a flurry of prosecutions.

A sympathetic Mussoorie SDM used his discretion and granted me bail, and a couple of months later I took the slow passenger train to Bombay, where I appeared before a very stern and apparently uncompromising judge. The case dragged on for a couple of years, during which I made sporadic appearances, once in order to plead 'not guilty'. In the middle of it all, the public prosecutor died of a heart attack. Those who had lodged the complaint which led to the criminal charge of obscenity gradually lost some of their enthusiasm. *Debonair* made a vigorous defence, and writers of the calibre of Nissim Ezekiel and Vijay Tendulkar spoke up for me in court. The judge must have seen some merit in my story, for he gave us an honourable acquittal. I believe a sixty-page judgement reposes in the archives of the Bombay courts.

Nevertheless, I'd been put on the defensive, and I did not publish the story again until Penguin India decided to include it in the omnibus volume with which they honoured me during their tenth anniversary celebrations. A literary critic remarked that it unveiled an interesting, complex aspect of the author, and hoped that there would be more in the same vein. It's a thought for tomorrow . . .

Landour   RUSKIN BOND
March 2009

One

When you hold him in your two hands, you should first honour him duly and then devour blin. You will find him with flesh upon his bones, but leave him as the remnants of a fish, which are spines and skin. But what am I saying? Even when there is no flesh left, you shall by no means cast the bones aside till you have cracked them and sucked the marrow. He must be left incapable of work, unable even to stumble, with wandering glances, emptied, broken, finished . . .

Damodaragupta, The Lessons of a Bawd,
(8th century A.D.)

This range is bare and rocky, with steep hillsides suddenly rearing up in front of the tired, discouraged traveller. The grass is short and almost colourless. An eagle circles high overhead and the burning sun, striking through the rarefied atmosphere, is reflected from the granite rocks. Waves of banded light shimmer along the dusty mountain path. I walk alone and I am thirsty.

The last stream disappeared into the valley ten miles back, and this region seems to be devoid of any kind of moisture. The villages, the terraced fields, have been left behind. The pine forests are a purple blanket on the next mountain. I have a long way to go to reach the river and the town. I must have taken the wrong path sometime back, but this doesn't worry me very much. I have lost my way in the hills before and found it again simply by following the line of a valley; but I will not reach the river tonight. It is already half-past three and the September sun is low in the sky.

I have a strong desire to sit down and rest but there is no shade anywhere except under the big boulders which look as though they might topple over at any moment. Huge lizards bask on the rocks, scuttling away at my approach. Where do they get their moisture? Some subterranean pocket of water must exist here to sustain these creatures, because except for the eagle, I find no other sign of life.

But this path must lead somewhere. There are no muletracks, no imprint of human feet to give me confidence, but no mountain path can exist without someone to wear down the sharp rocks and prevent the grass from growing. Someone, at some time, must pass this way, and beyond the next hill there should be a village and grass that is green; perhaps a lime tree with a patch of fragrant shade and a glass of sour curds and a draw at the hookah.

Even while I dream of it, I find a patch of emerald grass at my feet, and trickling through it a sliver of clear water. It comes from a rock in the hillside. Just below the rock the water runs into a small pool made by the human hand, and it is the overflow from this that runs across the path. I drink from the little pool and find the water cool and sweet. I splash my face and let the water run down my neck and arms. Then, looking up, I notice a cave high up on the hillside, with the narrowest of paths leading up to it. There will be shade there and a place to rest.

I clamber up the steep path. The dazzling sun leaps on me like a beast of prey, but I climb higher with the aid of rocks and tufts of grass. The sky turns round and round. Never has it looked so blue.

There is someone squatting, crouching at the entrance to the cave. As the sun is in my eyes, I cannot be sure if the creature is human or animal. It doesn't move. It is black and almost formless.

But as I come nearer, it takes the shape of a man.

He is naked except for a tightly wound loincloth. Long, matted hair falls below his shoulders. The ribs show through his chest. His skin has been burnt black by the sun and toughened into old leather by the dry wind that sweeps across the mountains. The eyes are bright black pinpoints in a cavernous face.

'It is some time since I had a visitor.' His voice is deep, sonorous.

I stare at this creature who looks like primitive man but speaks like an angel.

'I lost my way,' I explain.

'I had intended that you should. In a moment of weakness I felt a need for human company, and sent my thoughts abroad to confuse the mind of the first traveller who rounded the bend of the next mountain!'

'I was certainly confused. I hope you will be able to set me on the right path again.'

'All in good time. Will you not sit down here in the shade? I assure you that I am perfectly harmless. I am not even an eccentric, as you might think. For that matter, I am not even lonely. It was just a whim that made me desire your company. I hope you don't mind?'

'No.'

I do not know what to make of him as yet. Here is a recluse who has obviously spent a long time far from the haunts of men. I do not expect him to think or speak like other men. I realize that my norm is not his, and that, living entirely within himself, he must have attained dimensions of thought that are beyond my reach. The question that troubles me is, 'Can he harm me physically?' I am not afraid of the power of his thoughts, for I have confidence in my own.

He sits in the dust, and as there is no sign of anything resembling a comfortable seat, I drop to the ground, some five feet away from him. It is hot sitting there in the sun, but the only shade is inside the cave, and I do not feel inclined to enter that place. Besides, it will soon be evening and it will be cooler.

Two

The recluse looks at me, sizing me up, and I recognize the eyes of one with hypnotic gifts. I look away from him, although I know that it is not necessary for hiin to look at me in order to enter my mind. This is purely a defensive reaction on my part. I can feel the weight of his consciousness and I am immediately aware that he bears no hostility towards me. No action or word of his can make me feel easier than the aura of hopelessness that emanates from his mind, communicating itself to me.

'I suppose you practise many austerities,' I say. 'I admire men who can withdraw from the world, from a life of the senses. But I am not sure that I would want to do the same.'

'You haven't had enough of the senses, perhaps.'

'Did you have too much?'

'Yes, but that was not the only reason . . .' He gives me an enigmatic half-smile and I wonder, how long has he been here, and how old is he? It is impossible to tell from his appearance. He might have been here five years or an eternity.

'Perhaps you are hungry?' he asks.

'No. I ate at noon. I was very thirsty, but the spring at the bottom of the hill quenched my thirst. What do you get to eat here?'

'I eat very little. My existence is not entirely supernatural—not yet, anyway—and I must sustain this body of mine a little longer. But I have managed to destroy my former interest in food, and my body gets along quite well on the nourishment it receives. It is a question of conditioning, I suppose.'

'At some stage in your life you received formal education,' I observe.

'Oh yes, a fairly good education, although I never completed a single course. The learning I acquired has made it all the more difficult for me to accept this life. I love books. Therefore I do not keep books.'

'But why? Why give up what you love?'

'One can't give up some things and keep others. To reject the materialism of this life one must reject even the pleasures of the intellect. Otherwise, accept it fully—as I did once—and savour the delights of the senses to the full. Don't do things by half-measures. I never believed in the middle way, in moderation in all things. It never satisfied me. I took every pleasure there was to take, and then, satiated, I took my leave of the world and all that it meant to me.'

'With no regrets?'

'With every regret.'

'Then, I ask again—why?'

'I can give you a hundred answers to your question, and all of them would be right, and yet none of them would be right. For there is not one answer, but many.'

He rises to stretch himself. He does so with a single elastic movement, without the help of his hands. There is hardly any flesh between his skin and his bones, but his skin is as tough as buffalo-hide. He must be impervious to wind and weather.

He looks out over the bare rolling hills and the valley and at the silver river twisting across the distant plain like some mythological serpent. It is the great river we see, most sacred of rivers. To bathe in its waters is to wash away all sin.

'Have you come from Kapila?'

'I am on my way there.'

Kapila lies on the banks of the river where it emerges from a gorge in the mountains. It is an ancient city, much favoured by the sages of old.

'The stones by the river are beautifully smooth,' he says. 'Once, picking one up I took it between my hot hands, polishing it with care. I did not find it round enough, and I threw it far into the river so that the water might rub away its angles for a few thousand years longer. To me, as to a stone, a thousand years are but a day.'

He sinks to his haunches again and his long hair falls across his shoulders hiding his face from me. Although he has rejected the past, he cannot help brooding upon it. We cannot destroy our memories until we have succeeded in destroying ourselves.

'Are you comfortable?' he asks.

'Not very, but I did not expect to find comfort here.'

'There are some old rugs and skins inside.'

'I am all right. It is cool out here.'

'The nights are cold. You will sleep in the cave with me?'

'I should be on my way.'

'You cannot reach Kapila tonight. There is no shelter between this place and the river.'

I do not say anything. I have a feeling that the cave will not welcome me. It has about it an aura of damp and decay, the sweetness of a corpse soaked in scented water. But at the same time I feel that if this recluse really wants me to stay, I will find it difficult to resist his will. Those who live alone can be very strong. Having mastered their own minds (or gone mad in the attempt), they have little difficulty in mastering the minds of others.

I see the pine-tops dipping gently on the next mountain, and a little later I feel the evening breeze on my cheeks. I am still young, and a cool uplifting breeze always stirs me to the marrow. It is the best aphrodisiac in the world.

Three

'The body of a woman,' he says, as though something of what I have been musing on has reached him, 'the body of a woman is an inexhaustible source of wonder and delight.'

I look at him with unfeigned surprise.

'Oh, of course I have finished with all that,' he says. 'That is obvious, isn't it? But, looking at me, you might get the impression that I have always been celibate. Nothing could be further from the truth. As a youth, I had an insatiable appetite for pleasure. It overrode all other considerations, I moved from one conquest to another in the single-minded pursuit of sexual pleasure. I suppose it was partly due to the woman servant who looked after me as a boy.

She had some crazy idea that I was gifted with supernatural powers in these matters. She gave me strange potions and concoctions to drink!

'She was a big woman with broad hips and flesh buttocks that quivered at every stride. Early every morning, even before the sun was up, she took me down the steps to bathe in the cold waters of the river. There was hardly anyone about at that time. Her huge, heavy breasts smelling of musk brushed against my cheeks as she poured the powerful waters over my head. She held me firmly between her thighs and laved my back with her rough hands. Later, in the small courtyard of our house, she would massage my limbs with mustard oil and with her fingers she would press at the root of my penis, a sensation both painful and pleasurable.

'Sometimes, when my parents were away, she would make me lie down with her, lie down upon her naked and mountainous flesh, and she would take my mouth between her heavy lips and thrust her tongue against mine. This kissing was always pleasurable and I never tired of it. I was a merry monkey, full of good intentions, trying to satisfy an elephant!'

'Stop!' I say, unable to control my laughter. 'Why do you tell me all this?'

'I thought you wanted to hear my story.'

'Did I say so? Well, I didn't think you would be so explicit.'

'Would you like a more romantic tale?'

'No. Carry on. Just so you finish it quickly and let me go my way.'

'Would you hear more of this woman who instructed me in the hidden arts of pleasure?'

'If she is relevant . . .'

'Oh, but she is relevant. She was the sorceress who helped me become, not a god, but a satyr! There has been no romance in my life, no "falling in love" as you call it—except, perhaps, once, oh yes, once! From the beginning I was trained in the art of seduction, in the art of extracting from a woman all that she had to give—exhausting her, drawing on her hidden resources, feeding on her like a vampire, until she had nothing to give and was completely destroyed. Of course I did not reach this stage at that early age; but already at puberty, I was working towards it, I felt certain powers growing within me. It was power that I sought, not simply the appeasement of lust.

'A man who lived beside the river taught me to concentrate, to channelize my thoughts in such a way that I could gain a measure of mastery over the minds of others ... every day, for an hour, I sat cross-legged on a smooth earthen floor and gazed steadily at a small black phallus placed a few feet away from me. As I gazed upon the stone, it seemed to grow before me, swelling and throbbing, and I experienced the sensation of having discarded my own sack of a body to enter the substance of the stone. It was only momentary. A spider crawling over my foot brought me back to the reality of my material self. Many hours of concentration were to pass before I could ignore the movements of spiders or insects.

'At home I practised before a mirror, concentrating on the space between my eyebrows. This was strenuous at first, and a throbbing headache would often result. But after a few weeks I found I could stand before the glass for an indefinite period, concentrating on the space between my eyes.

'I concentrated on sounds. I could close my eyes, admit into my mind one sound—the tinkling of a bell, or the dip of a tap—and live with that sound, to the exclusion of all else. After some time, the tinkle would become the clanging of many great bells or the drip of the tap would be a thunderous waterfall. I had to be shaken out of the trances I had entered. My mother was worried about my strange behaviour. My father, whose many business interests absorbed his own sexual drive, could not be bothered. Only the woman servant, my mentor and aide, was pleased. Who was she and where did she come from? Nobody seemed to know. She had come to our house soon after I was born and had made herself so useful that my parents kept her even after I was long past my childhood. She had no children of her own but it was said that she had been married once, that her husband had died and left her very rich and that she had squandered her money on some obscure cult. The more orthodox did not recognize this cult and associated it with sorcery.'

'Well, it was sorcery of a kind.'

'Slowly I was developing my adolescent will to a point where I could impose it on others. I found it easier to do this when I closed my eyes. Then I could shut out all visual distractions and direct my thoughts towards the person I wished to influence. The first time I succeeded in doing this I thought it was purely accidental. Perhaps it was, that first time; but its success gave me confidence in my growing powers.

'It was a warm, languid afternoon and I felt the slow turning of desire as I lay on the string cot in the bedroom. Through the half-open door I could see our servant stretched out on her cot, her waist bare, her hair loose, her lips slightly parted, her eyes only half-closed. (Even when she was sound asleep, her eyes were never completely closed.) Desire welled up within me. I longed for her harsh kisses and rough caresses. But nothing was possible with my mother present, and I found myself wishing that I could be so gifted with magic powers that I would be able to make people disappear (or appear) at will! This, I knew, could only be achieved after hundreds of years of training, and one had first to learn to live a hundred years! Our thoughts are so tame and timid to begin with that we seldom realize, until it is too late, what concentrated powers lie untapped in our minds. And for those who learn too quickly, there is madness . . .

'But I turned towards my mother, and closing my eyes, directed my thoughts at her, willing her to leave the room, the house—go anywhere, do anything, until I willed her back again. For five minutes I assaulted her in this way, and when I opened my eyes I found her staring at me with a rather bewildered expression.

'"What time is it?" I asked.

'She glanced at the small gold watch on her wrist and said, "It is only three . . . Is there anything you want?"

'"No, but you asked me to remind you to go out at three o'clock." She had not made such a request but did not seem surprised at the suggestion. She got up slowly, stretched herself and went to the mirror to arrange her hair.

'"I have to go out at three," she said. "But I forget what I wanted . . ."

'"You were to visit someone."

'"Yes, that's it. Thank you for reminding me. It's your cousin Samyukta's birthday. Would you like to accompany me? They are always asking about you."

'"No. I do not like them. Besides, I have a headache."

'"Then I will wake Mulia and tell her to press your forehead."

'"It's all right, Mother. I will wake her myself when you have gone. Let her sleep a little longer."

'Mulia had been awake for some time and she came to me as soon as my mother left the house and began pressing my forehead, rubbing her thumbs over my eyelids and then pressing gently down on my temples. I let her do this for some time. I did have a headache, due perhaps to the effort I had made in shifting my mother from the house! It soon went, however, thanks to Mulia's ministrations.

'The voluptuous creature soon stood before me in all her monstrous beauty, a feast for the eye, a mountain worthy of conquest. I have never understood the misguided attitude of most people to heavy, fleshy women, who are generally considered ugly. Surely, in the generous abundance of their flesh, their broad dips and curves and gradual inclines—bodies where the questing lover may wander freely and unhindered, where he can stop and rest, or turn a corner and discover some hidden recess— surely these magnificient women have a marked superiority over those of a more conventional build? They have so much more to offer!

'Why go into detail? The memory no longer excites me and would only disturb your own peace of mind. I'm only trying to give you some idea of my development as a destructive force. Suffice it to say that my former governess was as thrilled as I at the achievement, and now declared herself to be my devoted paramour.

'Nor was it simply a matter of having qualified as a lover. The physical conquest was only half the victory. It could not have been achieved so completely without my having gained some command over her personality. Mulia had of course always intended that I should be hers. In spite of her imposing proportions, the strength of her arm and her delightful witchcraft, her instincts were truly feminine. She had sought to conquer me only in order that she might be conquered. I had yet to impose my will on someone who resisted it. I had yet to enslave someone who held me in hatred and contempt. That would be the real challenge—the conquest, the ego-destruction of someone who had so far remained inviolate!'

Four

'I must go now,' I say. 'It is not yet dark. I can be at the river before ten o'clock.'

'I advise you to stay,' urges my 'host'. 'It is not safe to walk these hills at night.'

'I am not afraid of wild animals.'

'Nor should you be, by day. But at night who is to tell which is beast and which is demon? For the evil spirits of these mountains, chained to the rocks by day, move abroad at night.'

'Do they trouble you, then?'

'They do not trouble me. I am too powerful for any kind of spirit save one—the spirit of an innocent! But come inside, it is getting cold out here.'

'It is dark in the cave.'

'I have a lamp. You have nothing to fear if you are pure at heart. Have you ever destroyed the soul of another human?'

'No.'

'Then what have you to fear?'

'Those who destroy souls.'

'Ah! Then you need not fear me, because I destroyed my last soul, my own, a long time ago.'

It is cold but dry inside the cave, which extends for some twenty feet into the side of the mountain. I sit down on a goat-skin and watch the recluse making a fire at the entrance to the cave.

'I will prepare some food for you,' he says.

'No, don't bother. I am not hungry.'

'As you wish. But I will light the fire to keep the animals away. Sometimes I am visited by a leopard or a hyena.'

The fire throws a warm red glow over his emaciated frame, and for a moment or two, as his shadow leaps across the walls of the cave, he seems a little larger than life. When he turns to me, his body comes between me and the fire, and he is now a crouching black phantom, featureless, faceless, formless, who might at any moment leap upon me in the dark to suck the blood from my fingers and feet. But his voice, as always, reassures me.

'Do you mind if I talk?' he asks.

'Not at all. I have no desire to sleep.'

'Nor have I. When I sleep, I am defenceless. Then my mind is invaded by sirens and beautiful women with twisted feet, and young maidens covered with boils, and they ravish me and I am helpless against them. By day, I am master of my own mind, and remembered flesh cannot touch me.'

'So you have not entirely escaped the world you left behind.'

'It is another world that invades my soul. Sometimes I sit up into the early hours of the morning, so that I may avoid these visitations. For when they possess me, they drain me of all my strength, as I once drained others of their life-blood. But I will not trouble you with a tale of torment. I will tell you instead, of the powers I developed as a youth, and what use I put them to! Did I mention my cousin Samyukta?

'I did not like her and she did not like me. We bore each other hatred and malice—and that was enough to make us physically attractive to each other.

'She was a pretty girl, but coy and very aloof, and I resented her airs and graces. I was never much to look at, and whenever we were in the same room she behaved as though I did not exist, although she was perfectly aware of my presence. She did her best to humiliate me. If she said anything, it was to comment on the careless way in which I dressed. But I was indifferent to my appearance. People were not impressed with me until I spoke to them or until they came within the ambit of my questing mind. Once I was certain of my powers, I could dominate most individuals; but certain barriers had first to be broken down.

'Samyukta and I were of the same age, and at the time I am telling you about, we were seventeen or eighteen. Mulia now called me her young stallion. But cousin Samyukta, unaware of my gifts, treated me with contempt and laughed at me whenever we passed each other on the road.

'I had always looked away at her approach, and that had been my mistake. But my joustings with Mulia had given me a new confidence in the presence of women, and I knew that my cousin, for all her supercilious ways, was not very sure of herself. One day I saw her walking along the opposite pavement, accompanied by two girls, school friends. Before she could notice me, I crossed the road and was standing in her way. She gave a start, but before she could speak (and her words were to be avoided, for they were as poisoned barbs), I fixed her eye with mine and held her motionless, while her expression changed from scorn to bewilderment to fear. At that moment, I am sure she felt I was capable of doing her violence. Later when we grew intimate, she swore that during that unexpected encounter she had seen a small yellow flame spring up in my right eye. I remember that she went pale, and when I saw her colour change I knew I had gained the ascendancy. I was so thoroughly aroused that I had difficulty in restraining myself from touching her on the street, in the presence of her friends. When I stood aside to let them pass, the colour flooded back to Samyukta's face, and she went strutting up the street, head in the air, as though she had just given me the snub of a lifetime.

'I smiled inwardly and walked home to Mulia. I told her of my intentions. She was not jealous. Knowing that she possessed my heart, she was prepared for others to possess my flesh.

'"But how do we arrange this?" I asked. "How do we get her here?"

'"We do not get her here. You go there, prince."

'"But she has a mother and an aunt."

'"They go out together on Saturday mornings. And on Saturday mornings Samyukta does not go to school. She prepares the midday meal, while her mother and aunt relax in the bazaar."

'"You are well informed, Mulia."

'She gave me a look of slavish devotion, took my hand and put my fingers to her lips. "You will never tire of me, will you?"

'"I will tire of you when you are old."

'"Ah! At least you do not try to deceive me."

'"You are not to be deceived."

'"No, but I am happy that you have told me the truth. I will preserve my burden of a body for another five, perhaps ten years, for as long as you desire it, and then I will go away."

'The next day Samyukta and her mother visited us. I did not make my presence felt, but sat quietly in a corner of the room, while tea was served. The woman talked about other women, the price of vegetables and the horoscope of a certain young man who might be a suitable match for Samyukta. My cousin sat between her mother and mine, saying very little, but occasionally casting a glance in my direction. Outwardly, I paid no attention to her, but after some time I closed my eyes, and conjuring up a vision of her face, dwelt upon it for some time, turning my thoughts towards her, creating a flow of mental energy that I hoped would reach her in waves of telepathic power! My intention, of course, was to impose my will on her in such a way that she would be absolutely receptive when the right opportunity brought us together. I wanted to be sure of her response well in advance.

'When I opened my eyes, I gazed full upon Samyukta. Her eyes were drawn inexorably to mine, and for more than minute we gazed intensely at each other, until even our mothers could not help noticing.

'"Why are you staring so?" asked Samyukta's mother, who was facing her daughter and had her back to me.

'And my mother, who could not see Samyukta's face said, "Do not stare like that, my son. You frighten me."

'My mother, a nervous creature, had in fact grown afraid of me during the past year or two. She could sense certain changes taking place in me without being able to understand them. She knew that Mulia and I were very close, and while she was relieved that I did not make too many demands on her, she was uneasy because I went to the servant woman with my confidences. Already dominated by my father, my mother was not one to assert herself in any way. She was content to put away money for my "future" and to make occasional donations to the temples. She was certain that there was only one way into the hearts of the gods, and that was through the hands of the priests.

'And so, because my mother was frightened by my look, I turned my face to the window. A band of hermaphrodites was passing by in the street. Just then I longed to be one of them, the perfect synthesis of man and woman.

'Could Samyukta and I uniting lose our genders in each other and be as perfect as the hermaphrodites? For a few moments, perhaps; and then, uncoupled, we would lose ourselves again until guided by the itching of desire, we took refuge once more in each other's embrace.'

'When the confrontation did take place about a week later, it came as something of an anti-climax. She was no novice. There was no pearl to prise loose from its shell, no citadel to lay waste. Even so, it must have been a novel experience for her, because she did not expect an assault as fierce as mine. She swooned away before the hour was up. I waited until she opened her eyes, and then I assailed her again, until she moaned and scratched and bit. I had expected to stain her bed crimson with my lust.

Instead it was she who drew blood. My arms and shoulders bore the wounds for weeks. Men have nothing to teach women. We can subdue women but we cannot teach them anything!

'Are you listening? Good. I am not trying to lecture you, nor do I wish to titillate you with an erotic tale. There is a principle contained in life that is more powerful than life itself. The body's rapture cannot be divorced from the rapture of the soul. It took me a long time to realize this. Certainly, at the age of eighteen, I had no thought for my soul. I believed in nothing, only love and its pleasures; and the strengthening of my mind and will was carried out with the object of gratifying my senses. I had no ambitions other than to glory in the delights that are there for all those who seek them—I was not interested in power or position. My father had money, and I was his only son. Therefore my first duty was to spend his fortune.

'My father, a man I hardly knew, had spent a lifetime in amassing wealth. He manufactured electric bulbs, shoe polish and a hair-darkening cream. (The same ingredients went into both polish and cream.) On those rare occasions when he entertained his friends, he liked to tell them about the struggles of his youth and how he hawked his wares on the streets of Delhi. Although he had never been to school, he was determined that his son should receive the best possible education. After I had taken my degree, he would send me to Oxford!

'The thought of spending half my life in college horrified me. I was determined to fail my exams in order that I might discourage my parents from sending me to college. My father had lakhs of rupees, and competent managers to run his factories. I would be quite happy to take the money and leave the factories in the capable hands of his managers—they would see to it that the business continued to bring in profits. I could see no point in hoarding wealth and believed it to be a son's first duty to spend money as fast as his father could make it.

'My mother seemed to think so too, because though she was frugal by nature, she tried to get me the money I needed for my clothes, rings, watches, entertainments and wines. She always gave me what I wanted, even if it meant dipping into her own allowance.

'My affair with cousin Samyukta was to last for over a year. But in the course of it I was to have several other adventures, some of them rather expensive. But I cannot dismiss Samyukta so quickly. She was a girl of some character, and when I look back on that wild and wilful time I realize that she had more to offer than most of the professional courtesans whom I visited from time to time. She did not give herself to me for mercenary reasons. I was a challenge to her own strong sensuous nature, and she matched my aggressive skills with her own passionate and fevered responses. She was one of those restless women whose physical demands can never be wholly satisfied. If I was with her, she was happy and satisfied; but if a few days passed and I could not visit her, she grew pensive, irritable, burning up in the fever of her own desire. We grew to like each other. That's strange, isn't it? Because we had never liked each other before.

'But of course there were a few other adventures.

'A youth of eighteen who suddenly finds himself a sexual warrior becomes quite rampant, and pursues his prey indiscriminately. Too indiscriminately for his own good. The pleasure houses of Kapila were few, and did not offer any very startling attractions. Most of the painted trollops were past their prime, and their patrons had first of all to be bemused with bhang or opium so that they did not look too closely at their battle-scarred partners.

'But there was one who was different . . .'

Five

'One evening, I pushed open the door of an old house teetering over the riverbank, and looked into a narrow passage dimly lighted by a green paper lantern. From within came the sounds of flute and sitar. A curtain was drawn back and an old woman came towards me. She was a withered old crone who glanced at me with an enticing leer and led me to the top of a staircase where she took my money with a swooping, gull-like movement. She then led me into a small, dark room where I was able to make out a wide couch, raised just above the floor and decorated with a gay but tattered rug.

'"I will fetch Shankhini for you," she said. "You will be happy with her."

'My eyes gradually grew accustomed to the dim light, and I was able to see the girl who entered the room and closed and bolted the door behind her. She drew near with a composed and friendly manner, as if I was an old acquaintance. And in some ways I suppose I must have been, for to the prostitute, all men are one—unity in diversity!

'Except for a diaphanous wrap of silk and a narrow girdle, the girl was completely naked. She wore white jasmine blossoms in her black hair. She looked little more than a child, although her hips were graceful and well-rounded.

'"Shall I dance?" she asked. "Tell me what you would like me to do."

'"Dance," I said. I had been unprepared for her youthfulness.

'And so she danced beneath the greenish moon of the paper lantern, and the only sound was the soft fall of her feet upon the mat. The heavy door shut out the music downstairs, the street-cries, the hollow boom of the river. It was a dance without music, without sound, and I felt as though those small feet were dancing gently on my heart, on the very source of my life. When the dancing ceased the girl smiled at me with an expression simultaneously wise, childlike and passionate. Looking like a sleek green-gold cat in the light from the lantern, she subsided softly on to the couch beside me. She had been trained in the art of making love. And yet beneath it all lay an undercurrent of innocence. I think this was because she suffered from no feelings of guilt. She had been brought up to please men as though this was her sole duty in life. She had not known and did not seek any other kind of existence.

'She did not let a moment pass in which she did not seem to be giving herself. Her aspect was continually changing. She did not surrender even one of her secrets without giving me an inkling that another still remained to be disclosed.

'"Do you find me beautiful?" she asked. It was her stock question. And I gave her the expected answer: "You are the most beautiful girl I have ever seen."

'She smiled at me with her large, childlike eyes. Then her head came between me and the lantern, and her face seemed to be framed in a halo of green light.

"'Forget everything,'" she said. "Here there is no time, neither night nor day."

"'Let me do something for you,'" I said, feeling suddenly generous towards this girl. "Let me give you something."

"'I take nothing,'" she answered. "It is for the old woman to take. You must only tell me that I am beautiful and that I have made you happy."

"'You are very beautiful. You make me very happy.'"

"'I have heard it a hundred times. But I still like to hear it.'" And then, drawing close to me and gazing into my eyes she said, "You are very important to yourself, are you not?" She raised her hand to my brow, and tapping my temples with her painted fingers, said: "There is a cold fire there! It is stronger than all other flames, and seems brighter. It fights against the warmth of the heart, and will quench the fire of many hearts. So you must always move from one to another. What are you looking for? There is nothing to find. Forget everything. Love me, and forget!'"

'Forget? Can the mind forget? It was written by a sage of old: "Remember past deeds, O my mind, remember!" But the injunction is unnecessary, because we are remembering all the time—even when we say we have forgotten. And can the memory of past deeds really shape the nature of future deeds? Man cannot help but live in conformity with his nature; his subconscious is more powerful than his conscious mind, and he cannot deny his body until he removes himself from the scene of all physical activity. It is useless to struggle against one's nature. Some believe that there is salvation in struggle—they are merely showing that they do not know what salvation is.

'At first I sought to assuage my restlessness by communing with nature. I searched for truth in the rippling of streams and the rustling of leaves; in the blue heavens or the wilderness of the jungle; in the behaviour of men, beasts and plants; in the superabundance of sunshine that pours down in India. But our bodies germinate as the resurrections of nature. Each bubbling spring, swelling fruit or bursting blossom, reminded me that I too was part of this burgeoning process, so that it was not long before the throb in my loins was as tenderly painful as the unfolding of a rosebud.

'I am not trying to give you the impression that those years of youthful dissipation were interspersed with a vague searching for my inner self. Once again, I have anticipated ... The search, if you can call it that, came later. I am merely trying to tell you how I came to be here. This cave is the end of all searching but before the search there was the indulgence, and the indulgence was a part of the process that brought me to this place.'

Six

'And meanwhile, I grew in Mulia's love.

'She tended me as a gardener tends a favourite plant, giving it all the water and nourishment it needs. Special sweets were made for me. Ancient recipes were turned up, and sherbets of many hues and flavours were given to me morning, noon and night. I had given up asking what they contained. I left everything to Mulia. She tried each portion before passing it to me, to make sure that the brew was not too potent. I was convinced that one day I would find her lying dead on the floor, poisoned by one of her own concoctions.

'But I was not the sort of person who could give anything in return for love. As soon as I found someone growing tender towards me, I withdrew into myself, became remote and cold, so that the love that might have been mine was squandered in an empty void. I was determined to leave them with a feeling of insufficiency. Those who gave themselves to me suffered for it. I became cruel and callous towards them. Was it victory I wanted, or the chance to spurn victory? Samyukta was made to suffer in this way. But Mulia, twenty years older than me, was an exception. I seldom withheld my affections from her, I knew that she was wholly for me and with me. My wealth, strength, welfare and happiness were her sole concern. I was the ruling passion of her life and I knew that if I was taken from her, she would lose the impetus for living.

'Shankhini, the woman who lived by night, was in a different category altogether. All men had immersed themselves in her, and she could not be expected to love an individual man any more than a man could be expected to love her. But what was the mysterious attraction that drew me back to her again and again? She had no hold over me. And the old crone who ran the house, certain that I was enamoured with the lithe and boyish figure of this unusual girl, put the price up at every visit. I did not care, I could afford it—or rather my father could afford it. It even gave me a sensuous thrill to hand over the money to the old woman. Not that the old woman excited me in any way; she would have found it hard to arouse a camel! But the business of handing over the money in exchange for an hour or two of personal possession, ownership, of the girl who lived always in green shadows, was a thrill in itself.

'But would I ever be able to arouse her to any degree of rapture? Although I restrained myself, and took the time and trouble to create in her some crisis of response, she seemed incapable of reaching a state of ecstasy and abandonment. There had been too many men, she told me. Coupling with them had become a mechanical process, and there was no intensity or pleasurable sensation in it. She went through the motions, expertly and in order to satisfy those who had paid for the pastime, but she could not be expected to enjoy the game herself.'

'So perhaps she was a challenge to me, and that was why I went to her. I wanted to elicit from her a genuine, not a trained response. I think she preferred me to most of her customers, many of whom were pot-bellied businessmen whose overburdened waistlines gave their manhood a shrivelled aspect. Obesity is not conducive to effective love-making.

'It may seem strange, but I liked to talk to Shankhini. In those days, there were few to whom I could talk freely. Mulia was illiterate, and her talk was confined to practical affairs, my needs and bodily functions. She had no other interest outside her small world of service. My mother was old-fashioned and superstitious and so we had very little to say to each other. I hardly ever saw my father. Fellow students at school and college considered me a snob, a wealthy aristocrat, a privileged member of a feudal society. They envied me, and were a little afraid of me too, because unlike others from affluent families, I made no attempt to ingratiate myself with them. Had I lavished money on a few young men, I would soon have had a following, but I had no need of sycophants. I could live with myself, and within myself, provided there were always these women to bear the burden of my ego.

'Samyukta was intelligent, but there was no real meeting of our minds—the relationship was purely sensual in nature. I gave her the satisfaction she needed after she had exhausted herself intellectually. She was studying medicine, and had to work very hard. Whenever she stopped working, she wanted to stop thinking. I could supply no intellectual need, nor was that what she wanted. But when I moved within her, she cried with ecstasy, she was convulsed with joy; but afterwards she had little or nothing to say. She turned over, lay flat on her belly, and slept.

'And so in the evenings, as the lights were lit in the bazaar, and pilgrims placed little leaf-boats filled with rose petals on the waters of the river, I made my way to the tall old house with the green paper-lanterns and asked for Shankhini.

'She was not always available in the

evenings. So I took to visiting her in the afternoons, when other men were busy earning a living.

'The old woman told Shankhini I paid well, and so she went out of her way to make me comfortable, to please me and to persuade me to come again. She did this as part of her duty; but it wasn't all commercial enterprise. As familiarity grew between us, we spent some time in talk. What did we have to say to each other? I don't remember much of it, but this strange girl had evolved a philosophy of her own to deal with the situation she found herself in. It was all a question of doing one's duty, she said. Death was a duty, just as much as life was just another way of dying.'

Seven

It has grown cold in the cave. While my ascetic host has been talking, using me as his confessor, the fire has died down. Outside, a jackal complains loudly, and the wind grows restless and rushes up and down the hillside, seeking entry into the cave. But we are well protected by rocks and overhang, and when this twentieth-century cave-dweller adds more sticks to the embers, the flames shoot up again, and the warmth reaches out to me and I reach out to the warmth, move closer, get up and stretch my limbs and then sit down again, while the man's eyes follow me with a bright, probing look.

'So far,' I say, 'so far, you have not told me anything very startling about yourself. You did nothing that would account for your giving up the pleasures you have described. I envy you some of your exploits, but they are not in themselves extraordinary. Many young men have visited prostitutes and have even found sensitive souls among them. And many young men have sought to go through their father's money. Some have sunk by stages into a hell of squalor and have been quite happy wallowing in their own filth. You did not sink very low. Your obsessions were not those of the pervert or psychopath. You were perhaps slightly more obsessed with sex than most, but apart from that your sex life appears to have been remarkably normal! Many young men would have done the same, given the opportunity.'

'I made my opportunities. I imposed my will on others. I cared for no one but myself.'

'I concede that.'

'And I am not even halfway through the story.'

'Ah, well, in that case . . . I have no desire to sleep, and it isn't midnight yet. You were talking of Shankhini, the girl with the green-gold body.'

'Yes. She preserved a perfect body, almost as a challenge and a taunt to the shapeless creatures who came to her by day and by night. She gave them their money's worth like a true professional. She was well-versed in all the technicalities of love making. She gave her customers her body but not her soul. She could not love men. Her love went to another, a dark girl from the coast who was also owned by the old woman. One day, entering the room unannounced, I found them in each other's arms, tenderly kissing each other. When they saw me standing there, they drew apart, unhurriedly and without any sense of guilt. Without a glance at me, the dark girl left the room.

'"You should not have come in without calling or knocking," said Shankhini.

'"There was no one about, and your door wasn't locked. Where's the old lady?"

'"She had to go out to collect some money. Sit down, and I will prepare some tea for you."

'I stretched myself out on the couch and asked, "Who was the girl with you?"

'"My friend. Why, did you like her? Would you like to go to her?"

"'I hardly saw her . . .'"

"'She is very beautiful. If you would like to go to her, I will tell the old one.'"

"'All right. If you don't mind, that is.'"

"'Why should I mind? It is my business to persuade you to keep coming here. If you tire of one of us, there is always another.'"

"'I haven't tired of you. I do not even know you as yet. But I thought you would mind because you seemed to like the girl.'"

"'I love her, but that does not interfere with our work. Men like you will come and go. Nalini and I will still be here.'"

"'Men like me . . . Am I like other men?'"

"'You want the same things, don't you?'"

"'No. Most men only want to possess you physically, I want both your mind and your soul.'"

"'I do not have these things to offer you. I think, I feel, but I cannot share my thoughts and feelings with any man.'"

"'You can share them with Nalini?'"

"'Here is the tea. Drink it, and tell me your pleasure.'"

'But after drinking the tea, I got up to go.

"You are very irritable today," I said. "I will come again." She looked dismayed and urged me to stay. Perhaps she was afraid that I might not come again and that her mistress would be annoyed. The old woman was just outside the door.

'"He would like to see Nalini," said Shankhini.

'"No," I said. "Not today. Some other time."

'It was a frustrating day. Mulia was out shopping. Samyukta's house was full of people. It was as though, for a few hours, I had ceased to exist for them! Although I knew that they were completely unconscious of my restlessness, I harboured feelings of resentment towards them. I was being neglected! I suppose it's the lot of the only son to feel that way.

'I must have given you the impression that as a youth I was obsessed with sex to the exclusion of all else, and that I was devoid of finer feelings. It is true there was a time when I believed that although all men were born equal, some men turned out to be more virile than others!

'As for falling in love, I had no idea what it was about. Loving (I was told) is giving, but at the time I was interested only in taking.

'Have I given you the impression that my life was spent entirely in the company of women? I had not made friends at college, but then, I seldom attended college. I found the lectures boring and a waste of time. I had nothing against books and even read some poetry, but I did not want life second-hand, from books. Mine was not a reflective nature—not then, anyway—and I could not reconcile mental pursuits with the pursuit of physical delight. And what would be the use of a degree in the Arts if I was going to spend the rest of my life helping my father to manufacture electric bulbs?

'When my father asked me to go to Delhi on his behalf, to attend an industrial exhibition that was being held in the capital, I agreed to do so. It was my father's intention to get me involved in the business. I was not interested in industrial exhibitions but I felt like a change from my confined life in Kapila and I set out with a sense of impending adventure. I had no idea where the adventure, if it came, would lead me. My father had given me five hundred rupees, and I would follow my fancy in seeing where it would take me and what I could do with it.'

Eight

'My train rushed into the darkness, the carriage wheels beating out a steady rhythm on the rails. The bright lights of Kapila were swallowed up in the night, and new lights—dim and flickering—came into existence as we passed small villages. A star falls, a person dies. I used to wonder why I did not see more shooting stars, because in India someone is dying every minute. And then I realized that with someone being born every half-minute, falling stars must be in short supply.

'The people in the carriage were settling down, finding places for themselves. There were about fifty of us in that compartment sharing the same breathing space, sharing each other's sweaty odours.

'At four in the morning I woke from a fitful sleep to find the train at a standstill. There was no noise or movement on the platform outside. It was a very small station, and the train for some mysterious reason of its own had stopped there longer than usual, so that those in the train who had woken up had gone to sleep again, and those few who had been spending the night on the platform slept on as though nothing had happened. This was not their train.

'I watched them from the window. A very small boy was curled up in a large basket. His mother had stretched herself out on the platform beside him. A coolie slept on a platform bench. The tea-stall was untenanted. A dim light from the assistant stationmaster's office revealed a pair of sandalled feet propped up against a mountain of files. A bedraggled crow perched on the board which gave the station its name: Deoband. The crow cawed disconsolately, as if to imply that this dismal wayside station was none of its doing. And yet—Deoband!—the name struck a chord. Wasn't this, by tradition, the most ancient town in India?

'The engine hissed, sending waves of hot steam into the fresh early morning air. My shirt clung to me. We were all smelling of perspiration. There had been no rain for a month but the atmosphere was humid, there were clouds overhead, dark clouds burgeoning with moisture. Thunder blossomed in the air.

'The monsoon was going to break that day. I knew it, the birds knew it, the grass knew it. There was the smell of rain in the air. And the grass, the birds and I responded to this odour with the same sensuous longing. We would welcome the rain as a woman welcomes a lover's embrace, his kiss, the fierce, fresh thrust of his loins after a period of abstinence.

'Suddenly I felt the urge to get out of that stuffy, overcrowded compartment, away from the sweat and smoke and smells, away from the commonplaces of life, from the certainty of my destination and predestined future. I would be a free wanderer, the last in a world where even the poets had retreated into the sculleries of their minds.

'I knew where I was supposed to be going: Delhi. I knew what I was supposed to do there—take the fatal step towards respectability. To be respectable—what an adventure that would be! And this prospect of an ordered, organized life frightened me. I knew that I could not put it off forever, but perhaps it could be postponed. I had five hundred rupees in my vest pocket. It would provide me with freedom for two weeks, perhaps three if I was not too extravagant. Five hundred rupees; the smell of coming rain; and outside, an unknown town. The combination was too strong for my wayward spirit.

'I clambered over my fellow passengers, my suitcase striking heads, shoulders, backsides. Grunts and curses followed me to the door. And then the train began to move. I was seized with panic. If I didn't get off quickly, I would never get off. I would be frozen forever into a respectable bulb manufacturer!

'I flung the door open and tumbled on to the platform. My suitcase spun away, hit the corner of a bench, burst open. The crow flew off in alarm. A dog began barking.

'The train moved on to Delhi, carrying with it six hundred souls in bondage, while I stood alone on the platform, in temporary possession of my own soul.

'The suitcase, which never locked properly, was soon closed. I looked furtively around. The coolie was still asleep—obviously no one ever got off at Deoband at that hour—or he would have grabbed my insignificant burden, carried it for a distance of twenty feet, and charged me a rupee. I needed my rupees. I could no longer scatter them about at random or live on credit as I did in my home town.

'I walked quietly to the turnstile. There was no one there to ask me for my ticket. I walked out of the station and found myself in a wasteland of nondescript shacks—some of them labourers' huts, some warehouses, one or two of them uninviting tea shops. The scene was a dismal one, and if the train had still been at the station I would have returned to it and gone to Delhi. But so far in my defiance of the gods, I had done quite well, and it would have been admitting defeat to have returned to the station to hang around waiting for another train.

'By evening I was still disconsolately on a small hotel balcony overlooking the street, telling myself that I was a fool. For three hours nothing had happened to me, and now it looked as though nothing was going to happen. There was no Mulia to press my aching limbs, no Samyukta to ravish, no Shankhini to battle with my ego. My only acquisition was a headache from drinking too much of the local beer and sleeping too long under the electric fan.

'The camel had gone from across the street, but in its place was a buffalo. The traffic had increased, there were more people in the street. There were also more flies on the balcony, and one of them came buzzing into my half-empty glass in an effort to drown itself in what remained of my drink. It was a suicidal kind of evening. I rescued the fly from my glass, placed it gently on the balcony railing and watched it crawl groggily away. But my compassion was wasted. As the fly neared the wall, a gecko, chuckling greedily, swooped on the insect and gobbled it up.

'There was no one to talk to. The hotel manager was a moron, and the bearer's thoughts dwelt on the contents of my suitcase. A large drop of water hit the balcony railing, darkening the thick dust on the woodwork. A faint breeze sprang up, and again I felt the moisture, closer and warmer.

'Then the rain approached like a dark curtain. I could see it marching down the street, heavy and remorseless. It drummed on the corrugated tin roof and swept across the road and over the balcony. I sat there without moving, letting the train wet my sticky shirt and gritty hair.

'Outside, the street rapidly emptied. The crowd dissolved in the rain. Stray cows continued to rummage in dustbins, buses and tongas ploughed through the suddenly rushing water. A group of small boys, now gloriously naked, came romping along the street which was like a river in spate. When they came to a gutter choked with rain water, they plunged in, shouting their delight to whoever cared to listen. A garland of marigolds, swept from the steps of a temple, came floating down the middle of the road.

'The rain stopped as suddenly as it had begun. The day was dying, and the breeze remained cool and moist. In the brief twilight that followed, I was a witness to the great yearly flight of insects into the cool brief freedom of the night.

'It was the hour of the geckos. They had their reward for weeks of patient waiting. Plying their sticky pink tongues, they devoured insects as swiftly and methodically as Americans devour popcorn. For hours they crammed their stomachs, knowing that such a feast would not be theirs again. Throughout the entire hot season the insect world prepared for this flight out of darkness into light, and not one survived its bid for freedom.'

'I had walked the streets of the town for over three hours, and it was past midnight. Shop fronts were shuttered, the cinema was silent and deserted. The people living on either side of the narrow street could hear my footsteps, and I could hear their casual remarks, music, a burst of laughter.

'A three-quarter moon was up, shining through drifting, breaking clouds and the roofs and awnings of the bazaar, still wet, glistened in the moonlight. From a few open windows fingers of light reached out into the night. Who could still be up? A shopkeeper going through his accounts, a college student preparing for his exams, a prostitute extricating herself from the arms of a paramour who had suddenly fallen asleep . . .

'Three stray dogs were romping in the middle of the road. It was their road now, and they abandoned themselves to a wild chase, almost knocking me down. A jackal slunk across the road, looking to right and left to make sure the dogs had gone. A field rat wriggled its way through a hole in a rotting plank, on its nightly foray among sacks of grain and pulses.

'As I passed along the deserted street under the shadow of the clock tower, I found a young man, or a boy (I couldn't tell which) sleeping in a small recess under a rickety wooden staircase. He was wearing nothing but a pair of torn, dirty shorts—his shirt, or what was left of it, had been rolled into a pillow. He was sleeping with his mouth open; his cheeks were hollow, and his body, which looked as though it had been strong and vigorous at one time, was emaciated.

'There was no corruption, no experience on his face. He looked quite vulnerable, although

I suppose he had nothing much to lose in the material sense.

'I passed by, my head down, my thoughts elsewhere—that is how we of the towns and cities usually behave when we see a fellow human lying in the gutter.

'And then I stopped. It was almost as though the bright moonlight had stopped me. And I started myself with the question, "Why do I leave him there? And what am I doing here anyway?"

'I walked back to the shadows where the boy slept and looked at him again. He seemed a very heavy sleeper, the sort of person who can fall asleep anywhere, at any time, oblivious to all that goes on around him. I coughed loudly, but nothing happened; I whistled, but still he slept; I picked up an empty can and dropped it beside him, but the noise had no effect on the sleeper. In his dreams he was elsewhere, moving among the spirit-haunted mountains, while his material body lay in this town. I found myself wishing that I could sleep like that—it was the sleep of one who was protected by his own innocence.

'I went down on my knees and touched the boy's shoulder. But he must have been touched often in his sleep. His lips moved slightly, but there was no alteration in the rhythm of his breathing.

'One arm was thrown back, and I noticed a scar under his armpit where the hair began. Looking at that scar, all the warnings of Mulia and my mother crowded in upon me—tales of crime by night, of assault and robbery. But when I looked again at the untroubled face, I saw nothing there to disturb me.

'And since he did not wake, and seemed comfortable, why did I not stand up and walk away and take the morning train to Delhi? I still do not know. Something was pressing me on, urging me to shake the boy out of his slumber.

'I took him by the shoulders and gave him a good shaking. He woke with a loud cry, as from a nightmare, and stared at me with something like terror. He sat up, cringing away, holding his hands before his face. But then, when he realized that I was a man and not the demon of his dream, his fear turned to indignation.

'"Who are you? What do you want?"

'"Nothing," I said, standing up and moving away. '"I did not see you there. I am sorry to wake you."

'I moved a few steps away, then stopped and looked back at the youth. He was still crouching on the steps, still staring at me, but he had lost both his fear and his anger, and he was only a little puzzled by this apparition in the middle of the night.

'"Haven't you anywhere to stay?"

'He shook his head.

'Perhaps the tone of voice I used gave him some confidence, because the hostility left his face and in its place I saw a glimmer of hope.

'I had committed myself. I could not pass on.

'"Do you want a job?" I asked.

'"No."

'"You have money?"

'"No."

'"Do you want some money?"

'"No, babuji."

'"Then what do you want?"

'"I want to go home."

'"Where is your home?"

'"In the hills."

'"Far away?"

'"Yes, babuji. In the Jalan hills."

'"And how much does it cost to get there?"

'"Twenty rupees."

'"And how much have you got?"

'"One rupee."

'He held his torn shirt in his hands. It was his only possession. I liked his open look, the way he returned mine without any attempt at evasion.

'"I'll see that you get home," I said. "On one condition."

'A shadow of doubt passed across his mobile face. (It was no mask, that face.)

'"Babuji—I have never done anything—anything shameful."

'"Shameful? You have not heard my condition. What did you think I was going to ask you to do—sleep with me?"

'He laughed and looked embarrassed.

'I said, "Don't be an ass. I have always taken my pleasure with women. Listen to my condition before you start getting nervous."

'He did not say anything but kept twisting his shirt in his hands—he was no longer looking me in the eye.

'"I was about to say that I'd help you to get home provided you took me with you. I would like to see your hills."

'His dark, sombre face lit up. He smiled like an angel. All the latent hospitality of his tribe welled up and burst through the barrier of his poverty.

'"Oh, I will take you to my home, babuji. I have nothing here, but in the hills I have a house, fields, a buffalo! Yes! I will take you to my home."

'No longer hesitating, he came to me, brimming over with a simple trust and joy. I could not betray that trust, nor could I fail to trust him. I was committed to a stranger in the night. I had sought him out deliberately, imposed my will on him and the consequences of the meeting would be entirely of my own making.

'And so there were two of us on that lonely street. The rain had held off just long enough for the encounter. Soon it began to drizzle.

'"We will go to my hotel," I said. "Have you anything to bring with you?"

'"Nothing," he said. "Yesterday I sold my shoes."

'"Never mind. Let us get some sleep while the night remains with us. Tomorrow, in the morning, we will leave this place. It has served its purpose, and now there is nothing to keep me here. Nothing to bring me back again."

'The boy lay on the mattress which I had removed from the bed and placed on the floor. His face was in darkness but the light from the veranda bulb fell across his legs. There was no escape from my father's bulbs! I lay flat on my belly on the string cot, while the ceiling-fan hummed in the moist air immediately above me.

'"Are you awake?" I called.

'"Yes," said the boy.

'"The mosquitoes make it difficult to sleep. So let us talk. Tell me, how do we get to your village?"

'"It is a difficult place to reach," he said.

'"Well, if it was easy to reach, there would be no point in my going there. Will we have to walk a lot? I have not done much walking."

'"We must walk about thirty miles. But first we must take a train or a bus. Later we walk."

'"Good. And now tell me your name."

'"Roop."

'"You have brothers and sisters?"

'"A brother, no sisters. My brother is younger than me and goes to school. I never went to school. There was another brother, but he died—he was attacked by a leopard, and the wounds were so bad that he died after several days."

'After a brief silence, he asked, "Why do you wish to visit my home, babuji?"

'"Because it is far away. Because I am bored with my own home. I have a mother and father and servants, but I am bored with all of them."

'Roop was one of those people blessed with the gift of being able to sleep sweetly and soundly through cannon-fire and earthquake. Once he fell asleep, there was little that could wake him. The morning sun embraced him, moved lovingly over his dark gleaming body, touched his eyelids, settled on his untidy hair. Still he did not wake. He slept on as though drugged. I called him, I shouted, I reached out and shook him by the shoulder, but he did not stir. A fly settled on his lips, but although his mouth twitched, he did not open his eyes.

'"One of us will have to get up," I muttered, looking at my expensive smuggled watch which showed nine o'clock. "Otherwise we won't get anywhere today."

'And I wanted to get away as soon as possible. The urge to stop at Deoband had been strong, but the urge to move on was stronger. During the night I had dreamt of pine forests and mountain streams, pale pink flowers growing in the clefts of rocks and fair hill maidens bathing beneath pellucid waterfalls.

'I got up and sprinkled water on Roop's face. Nothing happened. I placed my foot on his broad heavy thigh and shook him vigorously. But he simply smiled. He was still dreaming—of a girl, perhaps; or possibly of the chicken we had eaten on returning to the hotel the previous night.

'I decided that I would have to use some more positive method of rousing Roop. Shaking him was of no use, slapping his face would have been impolite. So I compromised—held the water-jug over his head and kept pouring until he awoke, spluttering and shaking his head and greeting the day (and me) with foul language.

'An hour later—my purse considerably lightened by our short stay at the hotel—we were sitting in a bus and moving hopefully in the direction of the hills.'

Nine

'It had been raining all morning, and whenever there were dips in the road, the bus sent up sprays of muddy water. Sometimes the rain came in at the windows and wet my shirt. But I did not close the window, it was too stuffy in the bus, and the reek of cigarettes and beedis added to my discomfort.

'Let us be grateful for neem trees. Their pods had fallen on the roadside, and these, bursting or being crushed against the wet earth by passing vehicles, emitted a powerful but pleasant odour which drifted in through the window on the breeze.

'The road was straight, but the bus was continually having to swerve or brake to avoid coming into collision with the slow and ponderous bullock-carts that came lumbering and creaking down the middle of the highway. In the fields, the ploughing had begun. Long wooden ploughs yoked between two bullocks raked crooked furrows in the softened earth. A heron stood on one leg in a rice field. An egret perched behind a buffalo's ear, searching there for tender insects.

'The buffaloes were of course in their element. With tanks and ditches overflowing, they did not have to search for muddy water in which to wallow through the long hot days. Some were already knee-deep among the water-lilies. Their dung, as always, was precious, and I remember the quaint spectacle of a farmer, realizing that one of his buffaloes was about to give forth riches, taking up his position behind the heaving beast and collecting a generous amount of dung in his arms, even as it fell. Hot and fresh it must have been! A second later, and this precious product would have been lost forever in the lily-pond.

'Yes, I remember that bus ride. Who remembers bus journeys? They are always so monotonous. But I remember that one, because it was a monsoon day and I was moving towards the unknown.

'The bus moved past a score of naked children romping in the rain; past a tonga-load of villagers, drenched but merry; past a young man with a dancing bear; past a sugar factory; past a railway crossing, mercifully open; past a dead cow, dense with vultures; past tiny huts and huge factory buildings.'

~

'I woke to what sounded like the din of a factory buzzer but was in fact the voice of a single cicada emerging from the lime tree near my bed. A faint light was breaking over the mountains. The morning air was quite chill, and I moved closer to Roop for warmth. We had slept out of doors, sharing the same bed.

'His mother and young brother, who slept indoors, had thought me a little strange for wanting to sleep outside. Most hill people prefer to sleep inside the small stuffy rooms of their rough stone houses, even when the nights are warm. It has something to do with their fear of the dark, their belief in demons and malignant spirits who dwell in trees or take possession of the bodies of leopards and sometimes humans. Roop told me that he had seen the ghost of a woman who had been at least ten feet tall, and whose feet faced backwards. His strong belief in demonlore made him reluctant to join me outside; at the same time, he did not want to have his guest spirited off in the night. It would have been impolite on his part to leave me to the tree-spirits. His natural sense of hospitality overcame his naturally superstitious nature, and he joined me on the cot in the bright moonlight. No electric bulbs in his village—I had escaped my father at last!

'Once Roop was asleep, he was immune to all the spirits of the dead, being even more comatose than a corpse. The shrieking cicada had no effect on him. He slept with abandon, one leg thrown over my thigh, an arm hanging down from the side of the bed, his head thrown back, his mouth open in disregard of his own warning that spirits enter people through the mouth.

'As the sky grew lighter, I could see through

the pattern of glossy lime-leaves the outlines of the mountains as they strode away into an immensity of sky. I could see the small house, standing in the middle of its narrow terraced fields. I could see the other houses, standing a little apart from each other in their own bits of land.

'I could see trees and bushes, and a path leading up the hill to the deodar forest on the summit. A couple of fruit trees grew behind the house.

'The tops of the distant mountains suddenly lit up as the sun torched the snow peaks. A door banged open. The house was stirring. A cock belatedly welcomed the daylight and elsewhere in the village dogs were barking. A magpie flew with a whirring sound as it crossed the courtyard and then glided downhill. Everyone, everything—except Roop beside me—came to life.'

~

'I was conscious of being observed. There was no one behind me, no one at the foot of the bed. But there was a soft football close by. I closed my eyes, pretended I was asleep. When I opened them, I found myself gazing into light brown eyes flecked with green—the fair complexioned face of Roop's younger brother. He had been looking at me with considerable curiosity because the night before, when I arrived, it had been dark and he had not been able to see me properly.

'When I returned his gaze, he smiled. He did not resemble Roop Singh at all, except in the sturdiness of his physique. He looked sensitive, reserved. The smile was shy, self-protective.

'"Is it time for us to get up?"

'He shook his head. "No, you can sleep. I have to go to school."

'"Your school starts very early."

'"It is very far," he said. "Five miles." And then, anxious to avoid further questioning, he ran off.

'The sun was up. It slipped across the courtyard and into the newly ploughed field and ran over the tips of the young maize that had come up with the first rain. It was time to get up.

'Roop's mother was a strong, handsome

widow of about thirty-five. Those with conventional notions of beauty would not have called her good-looking. Some would have thought her ugly. Huge silver earrings passed through the tops of her ears, turning them inwards, elongating them, twisting them out of their natural shape. Those huge, imprisoned ears were inclined to divert one's attention from the rest of her face. The forehead was narrow, but the eyes were large and attractive. The nose was a strong one, having withstood the weight of another large silver ring. She wore a silver bracelet and silver bangles clashed at her ankles. All her savings had gone into silver ornaments. It wasn't safe to wear or keep gold.

'Her voice was deep and resonant without actually being masculine in tone. She had strong hands, large heavy feet—she walked barefoot even on the rocky hillsides.

'Roop was rather afraid of her. The younger brother loved her deeply.

'She gave us a heavy breakfast of curds and black *mandwa* bread and hot sweet tea.

'She did not look directly at me, but all the time I felt that she was watching me.'

Ten

'I was to be enslaved by this woman in a way that no woman had ever been enslaved by me. As the days passed, I became aware of her strange and powerful matriarchal passion. It was not the passive worship of Mulia, but something quite different.

'Strangely enough, I had not at first thought of her in terms of passion. Her physique did not attract me. True, Mulia was strong too, but that was because she was heavy, a mountain of flesh; otherwise she was a soft, feminine creature. But there was no surplus flesh on this woman of the mountains. She was hard, even muscular. Her feet were longer and much broader than mine. Her legs, which I glimpsed whenever she climbed the steep path to the fields, were the legs of an athlete. She had strong arms and lifted sacks of grass or bags of grain with an ease and facility that would have been the envy of most men.

'There was nothing delicate or pretty about her, but her face was strong and handsome, and her eyes, although lacking tenderness, were expressive and of dark spiritual intensity. She laboured more like a pack-mule than a man, but there were powerful, unquenched fires smouldering within her.

'Three days passed before she spoke to me, and then it was to ask me if I felt tired. Roop and I had returned after a long walk to a famous waterfall. We came back very hungry and with our limbs aching from the effort of climbing up two steep valleys. His mother prepared tea for us and when she handed my glass to me, she looked straight into my eyes and asked, "Are you tired?"

'"Yes," I said. "Very tired."

'"Tomorrow you will rest."

'It rained heavily that night and all next morning.

'Only at noon did the clouds begin to break

up and then the sun came through, gleaming gold on the green slopes. I remember a flock of parrots swooping low over the house, their wings flashing red and gold and blue. They settled in the oak trees. Roop Singh had gone to the next village, where there was a shop, to buy salt and soap.

'I walked through the fields till I came to a grassy slope. Then the sun seduced me, and I took off my clothes and lay stretched out on the grass. I fell asleep—for how long, I could not tell—but when I woke, I felt curiously relaxed, languid, even light-headed. I passed my hand over my forehead and felt something sticky; then, looking at my hand, I found it was covered with bright red blood.

'I sat up, and got the fright of my life. My entire body was covered with leeches.

'They had crawled on to me while I was sleeping, had fastened on to my succulent flesh—as you must know, the bite of the leech can hardly be felt—and had then proceeded to gorge themselves on my blood. I now had about thirty leeches on my face, arms, chest, belly, backside and legs. One or two had had their fill and fallen off, leaving tiny punctures from which the blood trickled freely. One particularly fat leech—it was about two inches long—was feeding near my navel. I tried to pull it away, but it was stuck fast.

'I remembered being told that it was a mistake to remove leeches by force. The bite sometimes became septic. They would fall away and dissolve if a little salt was applied.

'I sprang to my feet, gathered up my clothes, and ran naked through the ploughed field until I reached the house. Seeing no one about I rushed indoors, surprising Roop's mother who was lighting a fire.

'If she was surprised at my condition, she did not show it.

'"Look, mother of Roop," I said, addressing her directly for the first time. "I'm covered with leeches. Give me salt."

'She got up from the fire, came nearer to examine me (it was always dark indoors) and said, "There are too many. Come into the other room, I will remove them for you."

'Armed with a container of salt, she led me into the next room and then started applying salt to the leeches. One by one, they squirmed and twisted and fell off.

'As they fell, they burst open and my blood oozed out of their slowly dissolving bodies, staining the floor. Little rivulets of blood kept trickling down from the open wounds on my body, which took a long time to close up.

'"I must have a bath," I said.

'"No. Let the blood dry on you. Only then will the bleeding stop."

'So I sat down on the floor feeling rather foolish, while Roop's mother watched me gravely from their doorway. If only she'd smiled or laughed, I would not have felt so uneasy. But she watched me intently, her seemingly dispassionate gaze taking everything in.

'It was an unusual situation for me. I had been in the habit of gazing upon the attributes of women. Now the positions were reversed, and a woman, fully clad, was studying my anatomy. I felt defenceless, rather as though I was a male spider or scorpion about to be first mated and then devoured by the female.'

⌒

'She came to me that night. I had been feeling the humidity and slept on the veranda, while

Roop, afraid of the early morning chill, slept indoors with his brother.

'I woke from a sound sleep to find someone lying beside me. Automatically, and from force to habit, I moved to one side. I stretched out an arm and my hand encountered those heavy earrings and twisted ears. Hastily, I drew my hand away; but I could not leave the bed. The woman's strong arms were around me, her powerful legs held me in a vice. Her breath, smelling of cloves, almost overpowered me.

'She did not attempt to kiss me. Kissing was obviously something foreign to her nature. But she began to stroke me with her large, rough hands; and aroused, I could not help but respond.

'This was a reversal of the usual role. She was active rather than passive in her attitude.

'Her breasts were huge pendulous things. Her arms and legs were much stronger than mine. Always proud of my virility, I now felt as though I would be inadequate for this woman who did not flinch, but who took me in her powerful arms and pressed upon me until I gasped for breath and wanted to cry for help.

'She did not give me any rest. She worked

on me with her hands until I was roused again, and then she mastered me with complacent efficiency. Nothing seemed to happen to her. She could not be satisfied. She was some kind of vampire, a succubus—I swear to it—and she was determined to drain me of my last ounce of manhood.

'Only towards morning, when first light showed in the sky, did she leave me, returning to her own room. I lay limp and exhausted. I had done nothing to quench her passion and I knew that she could overpower me again at the first opportunity.'

Eleven

During our long vigil in the cave, the fire has gradually died down. It is about four in the morning, and a faint light appears on the snow of the Bandarpoonch massif. I am feeling cold; but with sunrise only two hours away, I am able to summon enough patience and fortitude to bear the gnawing discomfort that has crept over me.

'Well—and then what did you do?' I ask.

'I ran away. Oh, not immediately. That would not have been possible. She watched over me wherever I went. She fattened me up with chicken and gave me strange sherbets to revive my flagging virility. It was Mulia all over again, but I was not the man who had tamed

Mulia. I was in the hands of a lioness, a woman far stronger, both mentally and physically, then Mulia had ever been. Whereas once I had imposed my will on others, I now found myself squirming under another's will. Roop's mother fed me on reviving herbs and fluids only in order that she might drain me of my strength. She was a *rakshasni* prepared to reduce me to skin and bone, to suck me dry!'

'And what of Roop—did he know what was happening?'

'He was too simple to comprehend. And he was too busy wenching with the village girls. He was a randy fellow, poor Roop. But the younger brother, he knew . . . He would wake up in the night, and tossing about restlessly, he would hope to disturb us, to put an end to the ravishing of my body. But she was in no mood to be bothered by minor distractions.

'And yet, there was a tremendous innocence about the way in which this single-minded woman had stripped me of my manhood and pretensions. Hers was the overpowering innocence of the mountains—I was helpless before it, just a computer lover overpowered by natural forces. She was not a scheming woman. She sought to appease a basic hunger, and she did so without a civilized veneer, without the cover of sophisticated talk. We who have grown up in the cities cannot understand the innocence of mountain people, because we cannot understand the innocence of mountains, high places which have retained their power over the minds of men because they still remain aloof from the human presence, barely touched by human greed. In the cities it is easy to despise those who live in awe of the mountains, because in the cities there are vehicles and noise and lights to hold at bay that fear of the dark which is the beginning of religion; but on the far hills the darkness is still terrible.

'And mountain people still keep some of their primal innocence. It can be disconcerting to one who is accustomed to the corruption of the cities, but unaccustomed to the simple terror and solitude of the hills, I was used to being the ravisher. I was now being ravished.

'Had another man violated me, I would not have found it as humiliating as the experience of being violated by this unlettered woman with the heavy feet and long twisted ears. It was not only my manhood that she stripped; it was my beloved ego.

'Roop's younger brother helped me get away. He had been in sympathy with me from the first, had sensed my predicament, my helplessness.

'Roop's mother had the custody of my suitcase which was locked in the storeroom. Having no need of any money in the village—there was nothing to spend it on—I had kept my remaining cash, about three hundred rupees, in the suitcase. I knew I wouldn't get very far without any money, and I was equally certain that Roop's mother would not give it to me—she had no intention of letting me get away.

'When the boy asked me, "Will you walk with me to my school?", I almost said no. The pleasures of walking did not appeal to me just then. But something in his expression told me that his intentions went deeper than what his words implied. He was not asking me to accompany him, he was urging me to do so.

'Puzzled, I said I'd come. His mother did not try to restrain me—she was confident that I would be back.

'We took the path to the stream, then followed the watercourse for a mile or two until that path forked, one branch twisting up the mountain on our right, the other keeping to the stream and running straight up the valley.

'"I will leave you here," said the boy.

'"Don't you want me to come as far as the school?"

'He shook his head. "No. You should go now." He opened the satchel which contained his school books, and took out my wallet. "The money is all there," he said.

'I took the wallet and thanked him; then I offered him a hundred-rupee note.

'"That is not why I brought it," he said.

'He smiled and started climbing the steeper path. Where the path went round the hillside he turned and waved to me. Then he disappeared round the bend and went out of my life—my first and only friend.'

Twelve

'Soon it began to rain. But I did not seek shelter. I walked ten miles in pouring rain until I reached the bus terminus. I was very tired when I got there and was tempted to spend the night in one of those seedy little hotels that spring up like mushrooms near every bus-stand; but I was afraid that Roop may have been sent after me, to try and persuade me to return. I caught the last bus to the plains, and the following day I was back in Kapila, secure among the anonymous thousands who throng the waterfront.

'My parents did not ask me too many questions. They were glad enough to see me back. At least, my mother was glad. She did not

have long to live and I think she knew it. She
had suckled and spoilt me and wanted to see me
happy. My father would probably not have
minded if I had disappeared for ever. He hadn't
much confidence in me, and knew I would
never be of any help to him in the business.
I've no doubt he was furious with me for having
wandered off on my own instead of going to
Delhi, but to humour my mother, he said
nothing. She thought I'd run away from home.
Now that I was back, she was ready to indulge
my every whim. Instead of getting less money,
I was given more. And if I did not attend
college, no questions were asked. No prodigal
son ever had it better. And in this way young
men are ruined for life.

'Although my mother adored me, under the
delusion that I was a favourite of the gods,
Mulia fussed over me more like a mother—or
rather, like a brooding hen. Who would have
thought that I was almost twenty . . .

'Strangely enough, I found that I had grown
indifferent to Mulia. Had she changed, or had
I? Had she grown older, flabbier, heavier, uglier—
or was it that I now looked only for the ugliness

instead of for the beauty? The strong odour of her body, which formerly had aroused me so easily, now failed to excite me. Instead I found myself disliking the odour. Strange, isn't it, how things that attract us become, after a period of time, the things that repel us . . .

'I spoke to Mulia as before, but I avoided being alone with her. If my mother went out, I found some excuse for going out too. Mulia was constantly seeking opportunities for being alone with me; I was ever alert, ready to slip away.

'Still, the confrontration had to come.

'I slept late one morning and did not know that my mother had gone out early. The air of September was warm and humid, and I lay on my bed in singlet and shorts, watching the lizards scuttle about on the walls. Then the door opened and Mulia entered the room.

'She had bathed, she had perfumed her hair and she looked quite magnificent as she stood there before me, with the sun from the open window slanting across her great quivering breasts. She lay down beside me and began to caress and stroke my limbs almost as though she worshipped my body. And although you may not believe it now, my body once had all the attributes of the perfect male physique. I was slim-waisted like a pipal leaf, with fine broad shoulders; and my thighs were like plantains, long and smooth and powerful. That was—how many years ago—five, ten, I don't remember . . . But it doesn't take long for a man to lose his vigour and freshness. Women and trees last longer.

'Anyway, to return to what I was saying, Mulia began caressing me, but I was totally unresponsive to her ministrations.

'"What is wrong?" she asked.

'"Nothing" I said. "I am unwell, that is all. I will be all right in a day or two."

'And I got up from the bed and went to the tap to refresh myself with a cold bath.

'That evening I bathed in the river. I felt listless and ill at ease, and perhaps I was hoping that the icy water would instil new life in me. Thousands bathed daily in the river. Each person sought his own cure, his own solutions, his own personal benediction; and that surging mass of human flesh appeared to me as one living entity, a shapeless jelly of throbbing amoeba, struggling for life on the banks of a timeless river. Was I a distinct and sacred individual, or was I just a part of the quivering jelly that sought cohesion in the swirling waters? And did help come from within or from without? Did it come from the mind, as my teacher once said, or was there really a potency, a magic, in the waters of the river? Bathing should be a rite, not a routine, I thought.

'Mulia was worried about me. She made me one of her concoctions, a bitter brew of *senna* leaves, rose petals, pomegranate-bark and laburnum seeds. The result was diarrhoea.

'I placed more reliance on Samyukta. A few hours with her, I thought, and I would soon be myself again. I had spent too much time with older women, and I needed the challenge of someone my own age. Or so I tried to convince myself.'

Thirteen

'Since my return, I had seen Samyukta occasionally but had not found an opportunity to be alone with her. Then one day her mother decided to visit a fair on the other side of the river, and Samyukta, pleading a headache, remained at home. I found her combing her long black hair in front of the mirror. I knew that she spent many hours at the mirror, and suspected that she was deeply in love with her own beauty.

'I began kissing her on her lips and throat, and presently she got up and undressed and came to bed with me. She had blossomed in the past year, and I think there were few women who could match her physical attractions. She had never failed to rouse me, to meet my challenge. She was prepared to do so now—even eager to please—for in pleasing me, homage would be paid to her own beauty.

'But something terrible had happened to me. My failure with Mulia was not a thing of the moment. There I was, lying beside a girl with whom at one time I had been brutal in my love making. And now, though there was no diminishing of desire, I found myself helpless, unable to take possession of her. For the first time in my life I found myself up against forces beyond my control. Fear crept over me. Had the woman of the hills completely destroyed my manhood? Or had my own body rebelled against me?

'The unfocussed stare of desire faded from Samyukta's eyes. She looked at me in surprise, and then in anger. My inadequacy was an insult to her beauty and womanhood. And she asked the same question that Mulia had asked: "What is wrong?"

'"I don't know," I said. "I must be ill. Or it's the evil eye."

'She got up and began to dress. She said

nothing. But her silence was more eloquent than speech.

'"I'll come again," I said, "When I feel better."

'How pathetic it sounded!

'And of course she said nothing. After all, what was there to say? A woman can hide her frigidity, but a man's impotence is obvious.'

'I primed myself on strong country liquor, and when evening came on and the sun sank in the river, and night crept up to cover our imperfections, I walked unsteadily towards the house with the green lantern and made my way upstairs. Shankhini's door was open. I walked in, but she was not to be seen anywhere. Feeling giddy and sick, I stumbled into the bathroom and, supporting myself against the sink, began retching. Then, exhausted, I leant back against the wall. And while I stood there trying to pull myself together, I heard the voices of two people who had entered the room.

'One voice was Shankhini's—I recognized it immediately. The other was a man's voice.

'They spoke together for a few minutes, then the bed creaked under their combined weight. I couldn't resist moving to the bathroom door and looking through the curtains. The bathroom was in darkness, but Shankhini's bedroom was brightly lit. She lay on her bed, a fragile figure, while her guest for the night took his pleasure.

'The man, a stranger in town, had close-cropped grey hair, hollow cheeks and skinny legs; he must have been at least sixty. But he went about the whole business with all the verve and vigour of a young stallion.

'I watched in fear and fascination. Fear for myself, fascination at the old man. I had fancied myself the world's most accomplished lover. And there I stood, finished before I was thirty, while a man who was more than twice my age performed wonders on a bed. My ego was shattered. My self-esteem lay in the washbasin.

'There was a door leading from the bathroom to the passageway and, unable to face Shankhini, I departed ignominiously, stumbling into the street and being sick again on the pavement.'

Fourteen

The clear light of a September dawn has spread across the mountains, and from outside the cave comes the call of the whistling-thrush, a song sweet and haunting, recalling for me a different kind of joy. But inside the cave it is dark and clammy, a home for those who despise the light—bats, rodents and hollow men.

All the awe I had at first felt for the recluse disappeared at the very moment that the sun came shouting over the hills. There is nothing more beautiful than daylight. I want to flee from the cave, from all within it. Renunciation? He has not renounced the world, he has hidden from it. And I wonder how many thousands there are like him—men who have run, not simply from the world but from themselves; men who, hating themselves, cannot bear to see their own reflections in the faces of other men.

He has produced a small chillum—a clay pipe—and filled it with the dried leaves of the cannabis plant.

'No wonder you eat so little,' I say.

'It is mental food I require. Those few or many years ago of which I have told you, when I thought that by strengthening my mental powers I might regain my manhood, I went again to the man who had taught me to concentrate, to bend others to my will. But he could do nothing for me. Perhaps he had lost his hypnotic powers in the same way that I had lost my physical powers—a failure of conservation!

'And yet this weed which grows all about me, has made life tolerable. It has so solaced me that in my fantasies I can experience all those sensual pleasures without my miserable body having to do anything! Surely that's an achievement—surely that's victory for mind over matter!'

'I wouldn't call it that,' I say, now ready to

refute. 'If it's the plant that brings you mental ease, that makes it a victory of matter over mind. Surely the only victory comes when the mind is free.'

'Perhaps, perhaps. But nothing else, human or divine, could help me. I had only one talent, you know. Misuse a gift, and you destroy it. And when I lost mine, I turned my back on the world and all it stood for.'

'But the world isn't exclusively a place for the pursuit of sensual pleasure.'

'No. But I was a sensualist. There was nothing else I could pursue.'

Before I go, I ask him where I can find the woman who had stolen his manhood—the hill-woman who had overpowered him with her own much stronger sensuality.

'Why?' he asks. 'Do you wish to lose your manhood too?'

'No. I wish to regain it. Or rather, I wish to discover it. And only a woman who can give so much of herself can revive true passion in a man.'